This Little Tiger book belongs to:

To Raven
Merry Christmas
From Santa

To my little sister Jess ~ *S L*

For the Irvine Chimps ~ *J T*

LITTLE TIGER PRESS LTD,
an imprint of the Little Tiger Group
1 Coda Studios, 189 Munster Road, London SW6 6AW
www.littletiger.co.uk

First published in Great Britain 2003
This edition published 2004

Yummy Yummy Food for my Tummy!

Sam Lloyd
Jack Tickle

LITTLE TIGER
LONDON

Far, far, far away in the middle of the deep blue sea were two small islands.

On Banana Island there lived a little chimp called

George,

and on Coconut Island there lived a little chimp called

Jess.

One day George saw Jess and thought,
"Wow, she looks friendly!"
And Jess saw George and thought,
"Hey, he looks nice!"
And they both thought what fun it
would be to share a banana milkshake
and a piece of coconut cake.

But there was a problem.
In the deep blue sea between
the two islands were . . .

. . . sharks!

" Yummy, yummy, yummy, food for my tummy,"

the sharks sang when they saw the little chimps.

"Don't worry!"
shouted George to Jess.
"I have a plan. I'll make
some wings from the
leaves of my banana
tree and fly across to
visit you."
George flapped and
flapped his new wings.
He jumped up and
down but he didn't fly.
" Yummy, yummy,
yummy,
food for my tummy,"
the sharks sang, snapping
at his little chimp toes.

"I've got it!" shouted Jess to George, excitedly. "I'll tunnel deep under the sea and come to visit you."

Jess dug and dug.
But the sharks heard the
digging noise.
"Yummy, yummy,
yummy,
food for my tummy,"
they all sang as they smashed
and bashed the tunnel with
their huge noses until it flooded.

"Never mind," called George.
"I've got another idea!"

Jess watched as George tied
slippery banana skins to his hands
and feet and started to ski-surf
across the sea.

Jess knew that this was the silliest idea yet,
but before she could warn him . . .

. . . he fell in!

"Yummy, yummy, yummy, food for my tummy!"

George swam faster and faster.
The sharks got closer and closer . . .

George made it, just in time.
"Well done!" called Jess.

Jess soon thought of a brilliant plan. "This will scare the sharks away," she shouted to George. With a mighty roar she jumped out from behind the tree, waving her arms around. But the sharks were not in the least bit afraid. They found the crabby coconut outfit very funny and began to roar with laughter.

"Yummy, yummy, yummy, food for my tummy!"

"This is no good," thought the little chimps. "We've tried every idea in our heads. We need to think of something new if we're ever going to share milkshakes and cake!"

They both climbed up
their trees – a very good
place to go when you
need to think.

As the chimps climbed
higher and higher,
the trees began to bend.

The higher they climbed, the more the trees
bent and bent . . . and bent . . . until . . .
"Arrgh, we'll be eaten for sure!"

Then, as if by magic,
the treetops met and
tangled tightly together
to form a huge leafy knot.
"Hooray, we're saved!"
cried George and Jess,
out of reach of the
hungry horrible sharks.

And they were together!
"Hi, George!" said
Jess.

"Hello, Jess!" said
George.

To celebrate, George and Jess
had a party with music and dancing.
And, of course, lots of banana
milkshakes and coconut cake.

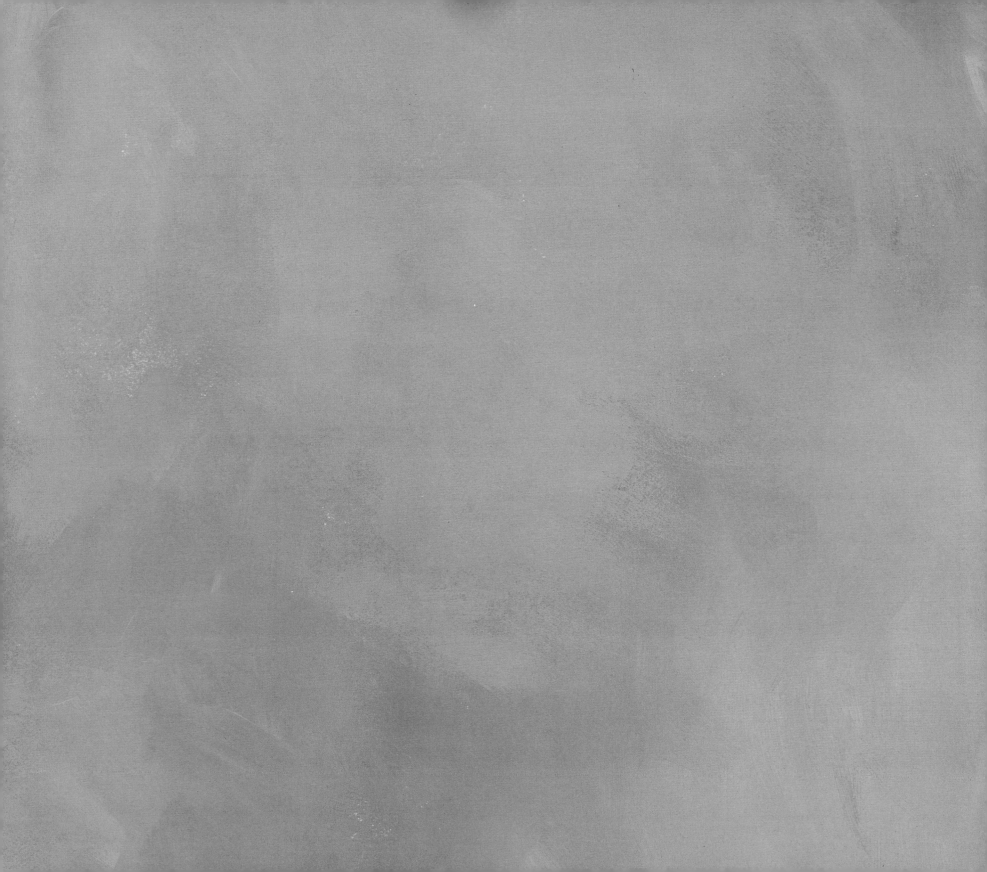